☆ Mimi's World ☆
Book 1

It's Not Easy Being Mimi

LINDA DAVICK

Beach Lane Books

New York   London   Toronto   Sydney   New Delhi

BEACH LANE BOOKS

An imprint of Simon & Schuster Children's Publishing Division

1230 Avenue of the Americas, New York, New York 10020

BEACH LANE BOOKS is a trademark of Simon & Schuster, Inc.

For information about special discounts for bulk purchases, please contact Simon &
Schuster Special Sales at 1-866-506-1949 or business@simonandschuster.com.

The Simon & Schuster Speakers Bureau can bring authors to your live event.
For more information or to book an event, contact the Simon & Schuster Speakers
Bureau at 1-866-248-3049 or visit our website at www.simonspeakers.com.

Book design by Lauren Rille

The text for this book was set in New Century Schoolbook.

The illustrations for this book were rendered digitally.

Manufactured in the United States of America

0918 FFG

First Edition

2 4 6 8 10 9 7 5 3 1

Library of Congress Cataloging-in-Publication Data

Names: Davick, Linda, author.

Title: It's not easy being Mimi / Linda Davick.

Other titles: It is not easy being Mimi

Description: First edition. | New York : Beach Lane Books, [2017] | Summary:
"Mimi and her cat Marvin must adjust when an unexpected new neighbor moves
into the Periwinkle Tower"—Provided by publisher.

Identifiers: LCCN 2017001400 | ISBN 9781442458895 (paper-over-board) | ISBN
9781442458918 (eBook)

Subjects: | CYAC: Friendship—Fiction. | Neighbors—Fiction. |
Schools—Fiction. | Apartment houses—Fiction. | Cats—Fiction. |
Christmas—Fiction. | Pageants—Fiction.

Classification: LCC PZ7.D2815 It 2017 | DDC [Fic]—dc23

LC record available at https://lccn.loc.gov/2017001400

For Tom

How It All Happened

Worse

Worser

Looking Up

My Friends and Me

Mimi

That's me! Even though I have a cat, a car, and a yellow sombrero, what I really want—more than anything in the whole world—is to have a twin. An identical twin.

Yoshi

is my smartest friend. He loves books and carries at least one with him at all times. The only problem is that he can't read yet. But he *can* play the ukulele.

Tonya

loves mirrors. She has a thousand combs and barrettes, and she always wears a tiara. She gives us lots of advice about everything.

Hunter

lives down the street. He's crazy about baseball. No one has ever seen his left hand because his baseball glove is permanently attached.

Sofie

lives up the street. She has so many after-school activities scheduled that she often falls asleep standing up. When she dreams, it's about horses and ballet.

Uncle Albert

is Yoshi's uncle who lives in Japan and sends great presents.

? ? ?

Wait a minute. Where did this guy come from? Does anyone know who he is?

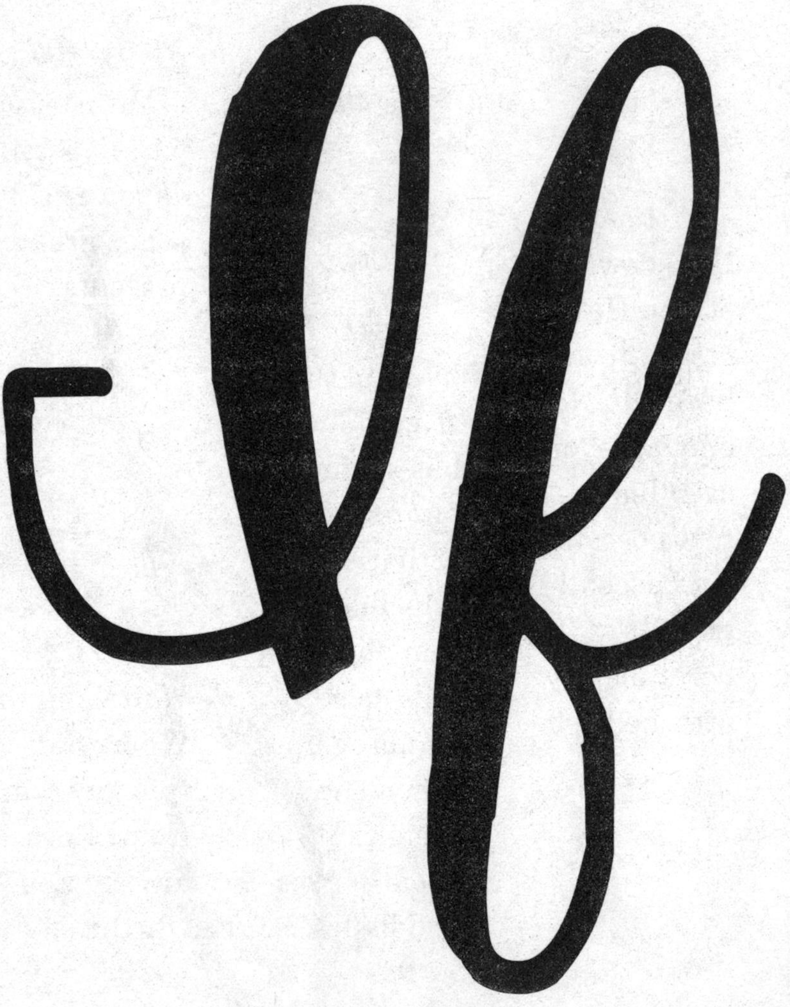

fly

The Periwinkle Tower

Hi, I'm Mimi!

I live with my cat, Marvin, in a tall apartment building called the Periwinkle Tower. It stands on a hill in a little town called Pueblo del Mar. That's Spanish for "village by the sea."

Marvin and I live on the top floor, in

apartment 4. Yoshi lives in apartment 3. Tonya lives in apartment 2.

Apartment 1 is empty, but Mr. Bosco, the super, says someone's moving in soon. I'm hoping she'll be someone interesting who likes doing exactly the same things I like to do. It would be so much fun to have a friend in the tower who was like an identical twin.

This story begins a little before Thanksgiving. That's when things started getting iffy.

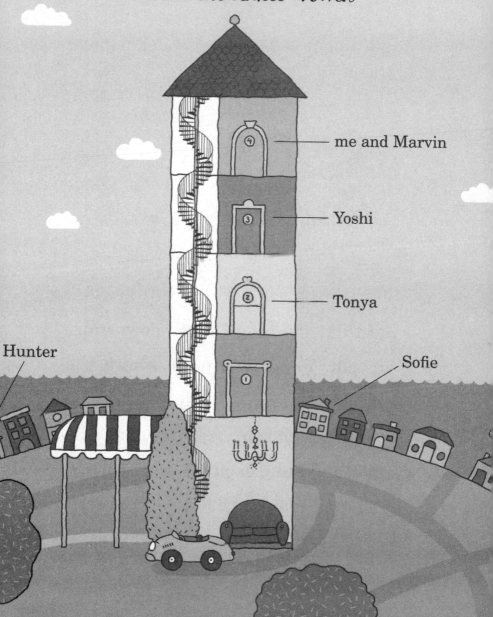

How I Got My Hat

Saturday morning I raced downstairs to visit Yoshi. I tripped where the carpet was coming loose and almost squashed Marvin. Yoshi heard the crash and flung open his door.

"Mimi, you need a haircut. You can't see a thing."

He got out his scissors and went to work.

Oops! One side was shorter.

He started over again. "Don't worry. I can fix it."

Yoshi trimmed and trimmed. Then he stopped.

He stuck his head out the window. Hunter and Sofie were digging a tunnel in the backyard, and Tonya was supervising.

Yoshi gave the emergency whistle.

"If anyone has a spare hat, please bring it up RIGHT NOW!"

Sofie, who was wearing her horseback-riding helmet to dig, was at the door in a flash. "But why . . ."

When she saw me, her eyes got huge.

"Mimi, this helmet will look

7

beautiful on you," she said, holding it out. But it was too small.

Hunter burst in right behind her. "You can borrow my lucky baseball cap," he told Yoshi, "but I need it back."

Then he looked over at me. "Oh." He handed me the baseball cap. "Here, Mimi. You can keep it." But it was not my color.

Tonya stuck her head through the doorway. "Is Marvin here? If he is, I can't stay. I'm allergic to cats."

Suddenly she gasped. "Mimi! What happened to your hair?"

Everyone could see that the tiara Tonya was holding was not going to help at all, but she made me try it on anyway.

I felt a tear roll down my cheek. Everybody just stood there.

Nobody knew what to say.

"Wait!" Yoshi said. "My uncle Albert sent me a hat. It's in my closet."

I tried the hat on.

It was perfect. Better than hair.

Tonya sneezed. "I'd better be going," she announced.

Sofie, Hunter, and Tonya cheered

as they slid down the banister.

"Bye, Yoshi!" I yelled as Marvin and I ran back upstairs. "See you tomorrow at your birthday party!"

Shopping

I had no idea what to give Yoshi for his birthday. He's the boy who has

everything, especially since his uncle Albert sends him great presents all the time, even when it's not his birthday.

The next day after breakfast I went shopping. I searched high and low.

Then I saw it: THE WESTERN BEAD BELT SALE. I hit the brakes.

Almost everyone from Pueblo del Mar had lined up around the block. They all wanted western bead belts.

By the time my hat and I had squeezed through the door, the belts were all gone! The cashier apologized. "They've been selling like hotcakes."

I was heartbroken. A western bead belt would have been the perfect gift.

Just then an angry man stormed into the store.

"This belt doesn't fit me!"

He held up the most beautiful

western bead belt I had ever seen.

Size small.

After the cashier promised to special-order a different size for him, the man calmed down. He left the beautiful belt by the register.

It was just Yoshi's size.

The Bucketcake

Soon as I got home, I slipped the western bead belt out of the tissue paper. Just for fun I tried it on.

A perfect fit.

I decided to keep the belt and bake Yoshi a bucketcake instead.

A bucketcake is just like a cupcake only much bigger. I mixed up all kinds of good things and shoved the bucket into the oven.

Then I lay down in a sunbeam to make Yoshi a birthday card.

The party music from downstairs woke me up. Oh no! What time was it?

I raced to the oven. But the door was already open, and the bucketcake was escaping.

The bucketcake was so big that I

had to scoot it out to the middle of the floor to decorate it.

Downstairs the birthday party was in full swing. It was time to dash down with the bucketcake. But it wouldn't fit through the door!

I pushed the bucketcake across the room and set it on the windowsill. I tied one end of my jump rope to the bucket handle and held the other end as tight as I could.

I gave the emergency whistle. "Happy birthday, Yoshi! Open your window and look up! Your cake is arriving by airmail!"

I edged the cake off the sill.

Everyone clapped and shouted as I lowered the bucketcake into Yoshi's arms.

Yoshi's Birthday Party

I skipped down the stairs to Yoshi's party, watching out for the torn carpet. Marvin had been invited too, and he ran ahead of me.

Marvin saw Tonya and headed straight for her lap. Tonya jumped up. "I'm allergic to cats."

Yoshi thanked me for the bucketcake. "I like your new belt!" he added.

Then Tonya said, "But it looks like a boys' belt."

I was so late that Yoshi had already opened all his presents. Hunter was throwing the baseball he'd given Yoshi up and down. "Think fast, Mimi!" He threw the ball at me, and it knocked my sombrero off.

"I'm still not used to your new haircut, Mimi," said Tonya.

She handed me a party hat, but I decided to stick with my sombrero.

Yoshi's uncle Albert had sent take-out containers of candy sushi for everyone. And after we ate the candy, we could each take home a pair of the colored chopsticks.

As I looked around for my candy

sushi, I saw a boy I didn't know.

He had a pair of yellow chopsticks in his right hand and a pair of purple chopsticks in his left hand. There were two takeout containers in front of him.

The boy was eating candy from both containers.

Boris

Sofie waved the toy horse that she had given Yoshi. "Mimi, have you met the new boy? Boris just moved into apartment 1 this morning."

My heart sank. This was not the twin I'd been hoping for!

"Hi, Boris. Are those my chopsticks

you're using? Purple is my favorite color."

His face turned bright red. "You can have your chopsticks," he said. "But the candy sushi is all gone." I picked up one of the containers in front of him just to make sure. Empty. Except for a big wad of green bubble gum stuck to the flap.

Yoshi set out a dish for Marvin and put a tiny piece of cheese on it.

Boris reached for the cheese, and I had to push his hand away.

"No, Boris! It's for Marvin. Cheese is his favorite food!"

Everyone talked at once. Sofie lit the candles on the bucketcake. At least I'd get to have a piece of my own cake.

As we sang "Happy Birthday," I studied Boris out of the corner of my eye. Four friends were enough, I decided. I didn't need a fifth.

"Mimi, this cake looks so good," said Sofie, after Yoshi blew out the candles. She handed me a big piece with lots of frosting.

"What are those lumps all over the cake?" asked Tonya.

"Chocolate-covered raisins. The best candy on the planet."

Sofie showed me the toy horse. "You can braid her tail if you'd like. Tonya, may we borrow your comb?"

Tonya handed it to me. I had just finished detangling the tail when a game of treasure hunt started, so I handed the comb to Sofie.

"Kitty, kitty, kitty!" Sofie called. Marvin acted like he didn't hear her, so she scooped him up. She ran the pink comb through his fur. "Look how handsome he is!"

Tonya screamed.

"You're using my comb on a cat!"

All in all, the party was tons of fun. On my way out Yoshi picked up a goody bag with my name on it. He looked inside the bag and frowned. "I'm sure there were some caramels in there with your chocolate-covered raisins. And now they're gone."

Boris breezed out the door with his head down.

My Bad Mood Ring

I scrambled up to my apartment and dumped out my goody bag. Empty caramel wrappers. A few chocolate-covered raisins. But wait! Something shiny and smooth clattered to the floor.

A mood ring! And did it ever look stunning on my finger. I'd always wanted a mood ring. I couldn't take my eyes off it.

In bed that night I got out my flashlight to check my mood. The mood ring was blue. Blue meant sad.

During the night I had a bad dream. In my dream all the cheese disappeared from the refrigerator. Marvin slipped out the window to search for more. I couldn't find him anywhere.

Monday morning I woke up late. But I was so happy to hear Marvin crunching his breakfast that I didn't care. I kissed him good-bye, opened the window, and slid down the drainpipe to my car.

When I got to school, everyone was folding paper and cutting out snow-flakes.

"Are we getting ready for the Christmas pageant already?" I asked.

"You mean the *holiday* pageant," said Tonya.

"Mimi, would you like to be in charge of the scenery?" asked our teacher, Mr. Dayberry.

I jumped up and down. "Yes!"

Painting was so much fun that I forgot all about my mood ring. I was just about to paint the star of wonder when

I remembered. It was time to check my mood.

Yellow? That was strange. Yellow meant careless. I wasn't feeling careless at all. Was something wrong with this mood ring?

I sat up. *SPLAT!* My foot knocked the can of paint over. Yellow paint oozed out across the field and fountain, moor and mountain. Not to mention my dress. I felt another tear roll down my cheek. Two tears in one week!

The Triangle

Yoshi grabbed the roll of paper towels off the snack table. We had just about finished wiping up the yellow paint when Ms. Marzipan tapped her baton on the door and rolled her piano into the room.

Time for music. I cheered up. I

glanced at my ring. Red? That was funny. Red meant mad! It was my turn to play the drum, and that always put me in a *good* mood.

But this time Ms. Marzipan let the new boy choose, and Boris chose the drum.

Tonya got a tambourine, Sofie got castanets, and I got stuck with the triangle. I do not care for that instrument.

"Boris, let's trade," I suggested. But Boris said he didn't feel like it.

We sang a song we had learned especially for the new kid.

"Getting to know you,
Getting to know all about you . . ."

With each word I got angrier. Finally, when Ms. Marzipan wasn't looking,

I pushed the triangle down over Boris's head.

"Getting to know you,
Getting to feel free and easy . . ."

And then the triangle wouldn't come off!

Boris told Ms. Marzipan he didn't want to stand beside me anymore. He didn't feel free and easy around me.

Ms. Marzipan finally got the triangle off Boris's head. Then she made me apologize to Boris and go sit down by myself. When Mr. Dayberry returned, I saw her whisper something to him.

Then he took me outside for a little chat. "Mimi, you're having one of those days. Please tell me this mood you're in won't last all week."

I wiped away *another* tear. "It's not me, Mr. Dayberry. The mood ring made me do it."

I yanked the mood ring off my finger and threw it down.

Mr. Dayberry smiled and took my hand. As we headed back inside, I looked over my shoulder. I had to check on the ring one last time.

Violet! Violet meant happy. For once the mood ring was right.

Ambushed Once

When I got home from school, I heard
a tapping sound.

I flew up the steps past Yoshi's door,
and there was Mr. Bosco, installing new
carpet. This time it was bright purple.

"Thanks, Mr. Bosco. That's my favorite color. And it's perfect with the periwinkle walls."

"I'm glad you like it, Mimi," he said. "Since I have to replace the carpet between your and Yoshi's apartments so often, I buy what's on sale."

I heard Marvin meow, so I stepped over Mr. Bosco's toolbox and headed on up.

But Mr. Bosco stopped me. "Mimi? There's something I've been meaning to ask you. The new boy, Boris, seems lonely. Would you consider making friends with him?"

"Not in a million years" is what I wanted to say. But instead I said, "I'd better go check on Marvin."

Ambushed Twice

It was a big mistake to have wished for a twin.

The very next day after snacks, Mr. Dayberry pulled me aside.

"Mimi, you and the new boy, Boris, seem to have a lot in common. . . ."

I could see Boris behind Mr. Dayberry's back. He was hunched over the snack table, stuffing the last of the cheese crackers into his pocket.

"What do we have in common?"

"You like to play the drums. Boris does too. And you love to draw. Boris loves to draw too. Would it be all right if he helped you with the scenery?"

I must have felt a tiny bit ashamed about what had happened yesterday with the triangle, because I said yes.

That afternoon as I was repainting the fountain, Boris walked over, dragging a humongous piece of cardboard.

"Mr. Dayberry said I could help you. I like dinosaurs. Is it all right if I make a stegosaurus?"

At least he'd asked politely, so I said okay.

Tonya wandered over.

"Mr. Dayberry!

Boris is making a dinosaur. Did dinosaurs visit the manger?"

"Mimi and Boris are the artists, Tonya. Let's let them do their job."

Mimi *and Boris* are the artists? I did not like the sound of that at all.

Green Bubble Gum

Ms. Marzipan had recess duty. We kept our distance.

Boris sat over on the slide by himself eating chips. I wasn't going to say anything bad about him; I wasn't, I wasn't, I wasn't, I wasn't.

Then I heard my own voice say, "Have you ever noticed how Boris smells like a submarine sandwich?"

"That's a *good* smell, isn't it?" asked Yoshi.

I couldn't stop. "Have you ever noticed how Boris always has crumbs on his shirt?"

"Oh, Mimi!" said Tonya. "I meant to tell you yesterday. You have a big wad of green bubble gum on the back of your sombrero."

That did it. I knew exactly whose gum it was. I marched over to Boris. He looked up and smiled.

"Boris, did you stick your gum on my sombrero?"

"Yes. When Mr. Dayberry came back to help me with my math yesterday. He thinks gum should be outlawed. I was going to pull it back off and finish chewing it, but you got up and left."

I yanked the bubble gum off my sombrero and stomped on it. When I tried to walk away, my shoe stuck to the sidewalk.

Accused

The bell rang. Ms. Marzipan waved her baton and began herding us back inside. I plopped down on the merry-go-round and took off my shoe. I tried to scrape the gum off with a stick, but the stick broke.

Ms. Marzipan walked toward me,

and I wondered if I should ask to bor-row *her* stick. I began to giggle. But then she pointed the baton straight at me and things turned serious.

"Young lady," she began. Those two words are always a sign that something bad is coming. "Yesterday you accosted Boris with your musical instrument. And today you're picking on him again. I'd watch my step if I were you."

My mouth fell open. This time no words came out.

The Invitation

Don't ask me why I did it. But Wednesday when I got home from school, I took out my purple pen and made three invitations. I slipped one under the door of apartment 3, one under the door of apartment 2, and one under the door of apartment 1.

Will you join me and Marvin for lunch at noon this Saturday? RSVP so I will know how many potatoes to buy. Your Friend, MiMi

Yoshi ran right up with his invitation and asked me to read it to him. Then he asked me if I would help him RSVP. I picked up my pen.

"Can you write it in another color

besides purple?" he asked. "Purple is *your* color."

I found a pencil and wrote down exactly what he said:

Dear Mimi,

YES!

Your best friend,
YOSHI

He folded up the RSVP I had just written, and when he left, he slid it under my door.

Later I found two more notes

under my door.

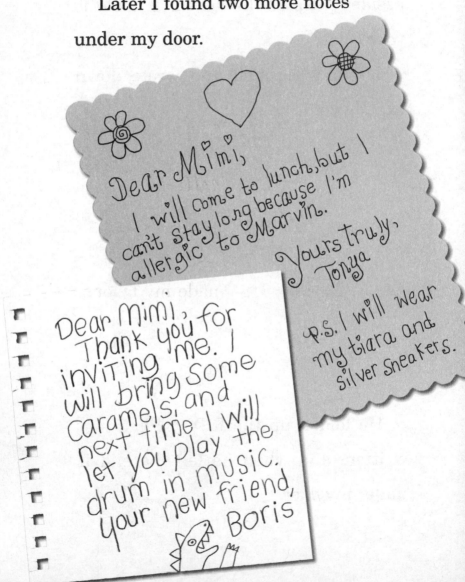

Dear Mimi,
I will come to lunch, but I can't stay long because I'm allergic to Marvin.

Yours truly,
Tonya

P.S. I will wear my tiara and silver sneakers.

Dear Mimi,
Thank you for inviting me. I will bring some caramels, and next time I will let you play the drum in music.

Your new friend,
Boris

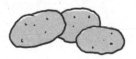

Potato Castle

Saturday morning I made my favorite
dish: Potato Castle.

The Potato
Castle
did not
last long.

Everyone wanted seconds. Boris even had thirds. Then he asked for the recipe.

Potato Castle Recipe
Ingredients:
1 bucket of mashed potatoes,
*   packed*
12 baked potato skins stuffed with
*   melted cheese*
1 extra large bottle of ketchup
100 French fries

Turn bucket of mashed potatoes upside down on platter. Remove bucket carefully. For windows, use potato skins, cheese side out. Pour ketchup around base of castle to make moat. Arrange fries around moat. Dig in.

After we passed the bowl of caramels around, Yoshi grabbed his ukulele. He strummed really fast. Tonya jumped up and started twirling. We all ate candy and danced like crazy.

Then Yoshi played "Somewhere over the Rainbow," and everyone slid down the banister and went home.

The next morning Yoshi ran up to my door and gave the secret knock. He brought his own pencil. He asked me to help him write a thank-you note, so I did.

This time it was a long note, and by the time we finished it, my hand was sore. I read it out loud.

Dear Mimi,

Thank you for inviting me. Did you notice that Boris ate more Potato Castle than anybody else? Tonya told me I needed to take ukulele lessons. I had fun, but sometimes I like it better when it's just you and me and Marvin.

Your best friend,
Yoshi

"Will you do it over?" Yoshi asked. "And leave out the part about Boris? It sounds mean."

"No," I said. "My hand is too tired. But I'll cross it out for you. How's that?"

That evening I found another note under my door.

Just as I was starting to feel more peaceful about life in the Periwinkle Tower, one last note shot across the floor.

Dear Mimi,
   Thank you for having me. I love to dance and I promise to teach you to dance better.
Yours truly,
Tonya

P.S. I left my barrette in your bathroom by the mirror. It is heart-shaped. It smells like peppermint. Will you put it in my mail box?

Tonya's Barrette

I called Tonya right away. "There's no barrette in my bathroom."

Tonya was silent. "You said you liked my barrette."

"I *do* like your barrette!"

Tonya didn't say anything.

Was this the Silent Treatment?

If it was, it was the loudest Silent Treatment I had ever heard.

"Mimi," said Tonya, "go look in the mirror."

"Okay. I'm looking."

"Is there a barrette in your hair?"

I took off my hat. "Yes."

"Is it in the shape of a heart?"

"No! It's in the shape of a dachshund!"

Tonya didn't say anything.

Sometimes being Tonya's friend is not easy.

Marvin's Brain

Something was wrong. On Sunday, Marvin didn't eat anything. And Monday morning he didn't feel like having breakfast.

I stuffed Marvin into his pet carrier and drove him to Dr. Furr's before school.

Dr. Furr listened to Marvin's heart.

He felt Marvin's stomach.

"I'm going to take an X-ray," said Dr. Furr.

I waited and waited and waited. Finally Dr. Furr brought Marvin back into the room and showed me the X-ray.

The X-ray didn't look like Marvin. It looked like a little dinosaur skeleton. But I knew it was Marvin. It was the inside of Marvin, and I loved every strange shape and every tiny bone.

"This is Marvin's stomach." Dr. Furr pointed to a shape on the screen. "There's something in there that shouldn't be."

I almost fell over. Could it be?

"It looks like
a little heart,"
said Dr. Furr.

It *was* a little heart. It was Tonya's little plastic heart.

I told Dr. Furr about the barrette that smelled like peppermint.

Dr. Furr said that he would have to keep Marvin overnight. He would get the heart out of Marvin's stomach.

"I guess you've heard that the way to a cat's heart is through his stomach," said Dr. Furr.

I was so relieved that I laughed at Dr. Furr's joke.

I kissed Marvin good-bye and stopped to look at his X-ray one more time.

I pointed to a tiny shape behind Marvin's eye. "What's that itty-bitty thing?"

"That's Marvin's brain," said Dr. Furr.

Dr. Furr and I laughed again. Marvin was not amused.

Wo

rse

Driving Steggo

On Tuesday, after the last bell rang at school, I skipped down the hall. I could not *wait* to pick up Marvin. As I flew around the corner I ran smack into Boris.

"Mimi, hi! Can you give me and Steggo a ride home?"

"I guess so, if he can sit on your lap. Who's Steggo?"

"Steggo's our dinosaur! The stego-saurus. I want to attach spikes to his tail tonight."

"Okay, but hurry! Marvin's at Dr. Furr's waiting for me to pick him up."

Boris reappeared dragging Steggo. Wo wedged him behind the seats. I started the car, but Boris made me get back out so we could rearrange Steggo. We stood him on his head. Boris wasn't happy with that, so we tried standing him on his tail.

"Let's put his front claws down with his tail sticking up. He'll fit best that way," Boris explained.

When I started the car again, Boris said, "Wait!" He climbed back out and stuffed his backpack against the claws for good measure.

All the way home Boris kept saying, "Slow down! Slow down or he's going to blow away!" It took forever to drive Steggo home.

Dr. Furr was locking his door when I finally arrived. "I'm glad you made it, Mimi! I thought Marvin was going to have to spend an extra night with us."

Dr. Furr brought Marvin out. Then he handed me Tonya's barrette!

Later, I gave the barrette back to Tonya. But when I told her where we found it, she said I could keep it.

Cheerio

The next morning Marvin ate his
breakfast with gusto. I
tossed the very last
Cheerio up in
the air and
gulped
it down.

I'd buy more on the way home from school. To remind myself, I grabbed my purple pen and started a list. Was it spelled "Cheerios" or "Cheerioes"? I wasn't sure, so I just wrote "Cheerio" on a scrap of paper and stuffed it into my pocket.

Because I'd driven Boris and Steggo home from school yesterday, today I had to drive them back. We were late, but for once Mr. Dayberry didn't seem to care. He had decided the class should have a pet, and today was the pet's first day.

A few of us at a time were invited to

come up and see. Mr. Dayberry asked everyone to speak softly to the little rat.

When it was finally my turn, I went up and whispered, "Hi, little rat. I'm so happy to meet you."

I looked the little rat in the eye and told him my name. "What's your name?" I asked. He didn't say. He just stared back at me with his sparkly eyes.

After we all met the rat, Mr. Dayberry passed out slips of paper. He asked us to think of a name for him. Later he would collect the names and choose one.

At recess I played on the swings

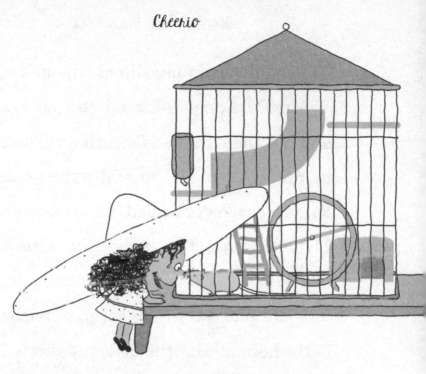

and thought about the little rat. He
was warm. He had eyes that twinkled.
He had a long tail without any fur on
it. He had whiskers and two tiny buck-
teeth. The teeth were so cute!

I jumped off the swing and wrote

"Bucky" down on my slip of paper.

Mr. Dayberry collected the names and put them in his bike helmet. Then he mixed them all up and pulled one out. He looked puzzled for a second. Then he read the little rat's name: "Cheerio."

I had put the wrong scrap of paper in the helmet! But the little rat seemed to like his new name.

Mr. Dayberry recognized the purple ink. "Since you named him, Mimi, would you like to be Cheerio's special caretaker next week?"

"YES!" I was super excited. Even

though Boris made me drive his stupid dinosaur home *again*. He wanted
to add silver claws to Steggo over the
long weekend.

Thanksgiving

We had Thanksgiving at Tonya's.

There were only six of us—but it seemed like thirty-six with all the mirrors in the room.

"Let's eat!" said Boris.

"First we'll go around the table, and each of us will say one thing we're thankful for," said Tonya.

Everyone slouched. But it was Thanksgiving, and we knew that's what we were supposed to do.

Tonya looked at Yoshi. "I'm thankful for my books," he said.

"Oh, can you read now?" asked Tonya.

Yoshi's face turned red. "Not yet."

"I'm thankful for baseball!" said Hunter, tossing a ball up in the air. It ricocheted off Tonya's mirror ball and landed in the cranberry sauce.

"Not at the table!" Tonya screamed. Then she clapped her hands. "Sofie, wake up!"

Sofie blinked. "I'm sorry. I had my ballet recital last night and—"

"But what are you *thankful* for?"

"I'm thankful for my horse. And my unicorn."

"There isn't any such thing as a unicorn," said Tonya.

"I'm thankful for Marvin," I said.

Tonya sneezed.

"I'm thankful for mashed potatoes," said Boris. "Can we eat now?"

"May I first mention something *I'm* thankful for?" asked Tonya.

We all sat up straight. Who knew what would come out of Tonya's mouth next?

"I'm thankful to be surrounded by my friends," she said.

No one said anything.

"That's you all," Tonya explained.

We relaxed.

"Let's eat!" repeated Boris.

Rat Duty

On Monday, Boris made us extra late. "Sorry," he said. "I stayed up all night working on Steggo's claws." The claws weren't quite dry, so Boris stuffed Steggo behind the seats with his feet sticking up. Then Boris climbed in and fell asleep on the way to school.

I didn't care. I was happy. It was my first day of rat duty.

At noon when all the other kids were in the cafeteria eating leftover turkey sandwiches, I stayed behind in the classroom to have lunch with Cheerio.

I jumped up and sat on the table beside his cage. I gave him a kiss and presented him with a special Thanksgiving rat platter: some chopped-up apple, a bit of sweet potato, and for dessert, sunflower seeds.

I polished off my own sandwich and sang to Cheerio while he crunched his seeds.

The Advent calendar was sitting on the other end of Cheerio's table. It had been driving everybody crazy all morning. It was hard to concentrate on your work when such a wonderful thing was right in front of you.

That afternoon some lucky kid would get to open door number one and take the treat. Maybe Mr. Dayberry would choose me.

I love teeny-tiny things so much. I wondered what kinds of treats were hidden behind the glittery doors. Charms? Toys?

Chocolate-covered raisins?

The clock said 12:20. Ten more minutes before Mr. Dayberry would return with the class.

What Happened to the Advent Calendar

I hopped down and quietly closed the door to the classroom.

You've heard the saying "When one door closes, another one opens"? The door I opened was the little one labeled December 1.

I held the wooden reindeer with the red glass nose up to the sunlight. My fingers were shaking, but they went right ahead and pried open the second little door.

Before I knew it, there were twenty-five teensy, bright toys lined up on the table. I could not stop staring at them.

Cheerio was under their spell too. He crept out of his cage and sniffed each one.

The bell! I jumped down. There was *no way* I'd be able to stuff the toys back into place, so I swept all twenty-five of them into my lunch box. My hands were still shaking, but I managed to seal each tiny door shut.

The instant I refastened the twenty-fifth door, I heard Mr. Dayberry's voice boom: "Slow down, please!" And then everyone stampeded back into class.

Uh-Oh

Later, Mr. Dayberry chose Hunter to open the first door on the Advent calendar. Maybe he picked Hunter because Hunter had made a fort for Cheerio to sleep in out of an old baseball cap.

Hunter swaggered up to the front of the room with a goofy grin on his face. He wiped his right hand on his jeans. It took him forever to open the door because of the baseball glove on his left hand. We all held our breath.

When the little door finally popped open, Hunter's face fell. "Mr. Dayberry? There's nothing there."

Everyone gasped, so I gasped too.

Mr. Dayberry frowned. "Open the next door, then, and take tomorrow's treat."

Hunter turned his baseball cap around backward. He took a deep breath and started loosening up the next little door.

But the same thing happened. Hunter's face turned red.

Mr. Dayberry jumped up. In an instant he was in front of the table. He whipped off his glasses and peered into the two empty compartments. "I can't get over it. Would they really have left out *two* treats?"

He picked up the calendar. "It's light as a feather." He shook it. "The calendar's empty!" Mr. Dayberry shoved his glasses back on and looked out at the class.

Everyone looked back in shock except for Boris, who had his head down. I knew Boris was exhausted from working on Steggo all night. But everyone else thought Boris was

sick. I could read their minds. They all thought the Advent calendar had been full of candy—and that now Boris was full of candy.

"Boris," said Mr. Dayberry. Boris's head popped up. Then he said,

"If anyone has anything to say to me after class, I'm available."

Confession

When all the other kids had gone for the day, I dragged myself up to Mr. Dayberry's desk. I held my lunch box behind my back and looked down at Mr. Dayberry's loafers.

At first I couldn't say anything. Cheerio leaped off his rat wheel and stuck his nose through the wire cage. I could feel his bright eyes watching me. The room was quiet.

"I'm listening," said Mr. Dayberry.

I opened my lunch box.

I pointed to the Advent calendar and started to cry. "It was an accident, Mr. Dayberry."

Mr. Dayberry shook his head. He looked me in the eye. "What should we do, Mimi?"

"I'll put them back right now. Is there any way we can just start all over tomorrow? We could have December first in the morning and December second in the afternoon. And maybe Boris could open the door for December second?"

Gold Tooth

The next morning everyone, including me, was relieved. The Advent calendar was back in business. Hunter loved the wooden reindeer with the red glass nose. And that afternoon Mr. Dayberry would choose Boris to open door number two.

At lunch Boris asked, "Mimi, can you give me and Steggo a ride home again?"

"Boris, why do we have to take Steggo home every single day?"

"Because I want him to be special. Mr. Dayberry doesn't give me enough time to work on him in class."

"What are you going to do to him tonight?"

"Give him a gold front tooth."

"Boris," said Tonya. "I don't think there were many dentists around when dinosaurs roamed the earth."

After lunch Yoshi pulled me aside

and said he wasn't sure stegosauruses had front teeth at all.

I exploded. "Why didn't you say so? Maybe then I wouldn't have to lug that stupid dinosaur home tonight!"

"Because Boris *loves* working on Steggo," said Yoshi. "What's so bad about giving Steggo a ride?"

"*What's so bad?*

"Boris makes me drive super slow, and I'm always late getting home. He eats all the chocolate-covered raisins in my glove compartment. He gets paint and glue all over the inside of my car. He's completely taken over my life with that big fat dinosaur.

"He just won't leave me alone!"

Yoshi backed away. "Okay, okay."

Wor

ser

Loitering

"Worser" isn't really a word, but it's exactly what happened. Things got worser and worser. Day after day I waited as everyone else in class got to open a door on the Advent calendar. And I can't tell you how sick and tired I got of hauling Steggo back and forth.

So I'll skip ahead a week or so. It was the day before the pageant. We would be having the dress rehearsal that afternoon.

At recess we watched the older kids crawl all over the school, hanging lights and tinsel. They'd been put in charge of dressing up the school for the Pueblo del Mar Holiday Decorating Contest.

"Why are they even bothering?" asked Hunter. "The reformatory always wins."

"Yeah, the reform school wins every year with that same lopsided star," said Tonya.

"The reformatory is where I plan to study when I'm older," I announced.

"Why?" asked Yoshi.

"Because they get to wear uniforms. And live inside a private compound."

"A compound surrounded by barbed wire!" giggled Sofie.

"And they all get to sleep

together in one big room. A big pajama party every night. I can't *wait* to sleep in the reformatory dormitory."

"I think they only accept boys," said Boris.

"That needs to change," I said. "I'm determined to be the first girl to get in."

The bell rang. We trudged inside. When we reached the cafeteria, we stopped and inhaled deeply. The fourth graders had been chosen to make a gingerbread schoolhouse. Giant cookies were coming out of the oven. The smell was yumma-licious.

Ms. Marzipan pointed her baton at us. She told us to stop loitering and escorted us to the auditorium for rehearsal.

Dress Rehearsal

Sofie was supposed to play the part of Mary, but she kept falling asleep at the manger. So Tonya got to be Mary after all, and Sofie was demoted to King #2. That way King #1 or King #3 could elbow her if she dozed off.

But Sofie didn't mind. Everybody

but everybody wanted to be one of the three kings. The kings got to wear crowns with jewels and carry presents to the baby.

Nobody wanted to be the shepherd, so I volunteered—under one condition: that Marvin could play the sheep.

Rehearsal went well. Ms. Marzipan looked up from the piano and beamed when the angel appeared. The angel glided onto the stage on her skateboard. It really looked like she was flying. And *tomorrow* when she appeared unto me, my sheep, Marvin, would be there, and I knew he would bring the whole pageant to life.

After we'd practiced the last song, I felt a tap on my shoulder.

"Mimi, will you drive our stegosaurus home so I can finish him tonight?"

"FINISH HIM? Look at him! He's finished!"

"He needs spots. And I want to spray shellac on him so he'll be shiny."

My eyeballs almost rolled out of my head. "Okay. But meet me at the car in *three minutes flat*. I've got to practice herding Marvin this evening."

Disaster #1

Of course Boris and Steggo were not back in three minutes. When ten minutes had gone by, I ran back in to look for them.

Steggo was leaning up against the cafeteria door, so I poked my head inside.

The lights were off, but the spicy baking smell still hung in the air. When my eyes grew accustomed to the darkness, I saw the gingerbread schoolhouse across the room. Guess who was standing there drooling over it?

I marched over and yanked Boris away from the schoolhouse by his shirttail. When I let go, he fell forward and went right through the roof.

"What's going on in here?" It was Ms. Marzipan.

Boris acted like he was hurt! He pointed at me.

"Mimi, if you don't practice better self-control, you're going to end up at the reformatory."

The reformatory! If I hadn't been so mad at Boris, I would have smiled.

Ms. Marzipan snapped on the lights. "Now I'm going to have to spend the next hour piecing the roof back together with frosting."

"I'll help you," Boris volunteered.

Ms. Marzipan just gave him a look.

Boris and I didn't speak the whole way home.

I drove up and parked by the drainpipe. Tonya and Yoshi were outside cheering and clapping for Mr. Bosco. We had each decorated our own window. And now Mr. Bosco was running lights up the sides of the Periwinkle Tower and under the eaves, too.

"Look! We might win the decorating contest!" Tonya twirled around and around and waved her wand at Mr. Bosco.

Yoshi bounded across the yard. "We might beat the reformatory!"

Boris and I stomped into the
building.

We did
not have
the holiday
spirit.

Disaster #2

The emergency whistle woke me. I jumped up and peeked under the window shade. There was Boris, leaning against my car. If Boris was waiting for *me*, it must be late. *Really* late.

I opened the window and reached for the drainpipe. A gust of icy wind hit me—and then I remembered: Today was the day of the pageant! I couldn't take the drainpipe down to the car. I had Marvin's pet carrier to deal with. And my sheep staff, too.

I threw my jacket on over my shepherd robe. As I carried Marvin down the stairs—one step at a time—I thought about putting the top up on my car so Marvin wouldn't catch a cold. But I realized there was no way I could do that with Boris's stupid dinosaur sticking out.

Boris could not wipe the grin off his face. He pointed to Steggo, leaning up against the tower.

And okay.

I'll admit it.

The stegosaurus looked magnificent.

But it took us *forever* to wedge him in. His tail was still tacky, so we finally tucked him behind the seats headfirst.

I set Marvin down on Boris's lap.
Marvin sneezed. Boris unzipped his
king costume. Then he removed Marvin
from his carrier. He settled Marvin on
his striped shirt, zipped his costume
back up, and wrapped
his arms around him.
My heart defrosted a
tiny bit.

As I backed down the driveway, the wind blew a string of pink lights off Tonya's window.

"Mimi, stop! Tonya's lights!"

"We don't have time, Boris! We are *so late!*"

By the time we got to school, my hands were frozen. Even though the wind was howling, we could hear Marvin purring next to Boris's stomach.

Boris and I actually shared a laugh.

I turned around to help pull Steggo out, but Steggo was gone.

"He must have blown away!" I said.

"Mimi, get back in the car! We've got to find him."

"Boris! *We. Are. Late.* We can't drive all over town looking for Steggo—we just can't!"

Boris handed Marvin to me and started to cry. I felt sorry for Boris. I might even have put an arm around him if I hadn't been carrying Marvin.

Baby Gifts

By the time we finally made it back-
stage, the program had already begun.
Mr. Bosco had hung a gigantic papier-
mâché dreidel from the ceiling. The
kids from the class next door were
making it spin. They danced around it
singing "The Dreidel Song."

"Where have you been?" asked Tonya when she saw Boris. She had been waiting to hold a conference with the three kings.

Now that she was playing the baby Jesus's mother, Tonya thought that gave her the right to inspect the baby's gifts ahead of time.

"What are you bringing the baby?" she asked Boris.

Boris wiped away a tear. He held up a bag of caramels tied with a ribbon.

"Boris," she hissed, "you can't bring candy to a newborn baby!" She tried to grab the bag, but Boris hugged it to his heart.

Tonya approved of Sofie's present, a stuffed unicorn. "The baby Jesus will love that one," she said.

Yoshi was eager to show his present, a big fat book.

"*Little Women*?" Tonya smacked her forehead. "Hello, Yoshi. *Jesus* is a *boy*!"

Yoshi's face turned bright red. "I

meant to grab *Little Men*." Yoshi took off his glasses and studied the cover. It was mean of Tonya to yell, because she knew he couldn't read yet.

"Don't worry, I'll turn it around backward," he said.

Tonya snatched the book away from Yoshi and rooted around in her purse. "Here, give him this."

"But Jesus can't use a hairbrush!"

Tonya snapped her purse shut. "It's getting hot in Bethlehem," she said. She marched over to the back door and used *Little Women* to prop it open.

Suddenly there was a huge

commotion. We heard shrieks of laughter, running, and stomping. I peeked out from behind the curtain.

It was raining gold coins! Those crazy kids were throwing handfuls of chocolate coins into the audience, and the audience was going nuts.

"Hanukkah gelt," whispered Sofie.

Backstage, we all looked at one another. This was going to be a tough act to follow.

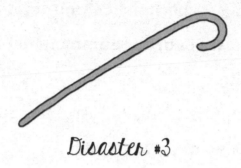

Disaster #3

The stage lights flickered. My stomach got fluttery. Then Ms. Marzipan began playing "Mary Had a Baby," and I started to get that good holiday feeling.

When Mr. Dayberry gave the signal, the curtains opened. Boris had punched holes in the star of wonder, and Mr. Bosco was up on a ladder shining a spotlight behind it. It made the most beautiful glimmer, just like a real star.

"Shepherd! Angel! Are you ready?" Mr. Dayberry whispered.

We nodded. It was almost time for the angel to appear unto me. I opened Marvin's carrier and fastened his sheep costume on. It was actually a diaper, but from the audience it made him look just like a lamb.

The angel grabbed her harp. "My wings!" she whispered. I stood and flipped them right side up. Then I reached down to fasten Marvin's leash, but Marvin was gone. I almost fainted.

I heard Mr. Dayberry read, "'And there was a shepherd in the field nearby, watching her sheep by night.'"

I was supposed to be out there already!

I grabbed my staff and raced onstage without my sheep, because the angel was just about ready to appear unto me.

As Mr. Dayberry read, "'And an angel appeared . . . ,'" Sofie gave a push and the angel glided up to me. When Mr. Bosco shone the spotlight on us,

the angel's eyes got huge. I could read her lips: "Where's your sheep?"

I was worried sick. It was dark backstage. Marvin's favorite game was squeezing himself into tiny, dark places and hiding. I would never find him. And what if he got outside? A storm was brewing. And cars did not always slow down for our school.

A Surprise

Ms. Marzipan raised her baton, and everyone sang:

"We three kings of Orient are;
Bearing gifts, we traverse afar,
Field and fountain, moor and
mountain,
Following yonder star."

The three kings strolled out and laid their gifts beside the manger.

After Mr. Dayberry finished reading the Christmas story, the curtain closed. We all managed to line up behind the manger in the dark for the grand finale. Mr. Dayberry made us hold hands.

Yoshi hopped up on a stool with his ukulele. He played the prettiest chords as the curtain swooshed back open. This time Mr. Bosco wiggled the spotlight really fast behind the star and made it shimmer.

We sang "What Child Is This?" The audience even joined in, because everyone was under a spell. I would have been under the same spell, only I had a stomachache from worrying about Marvin.

When we got to the last line, "The Babe, the Son of Mary," Mr. Bosco shone the spotlight directly on the manger. He made the light get brighter and brighter and brighter.

The baby Jesus

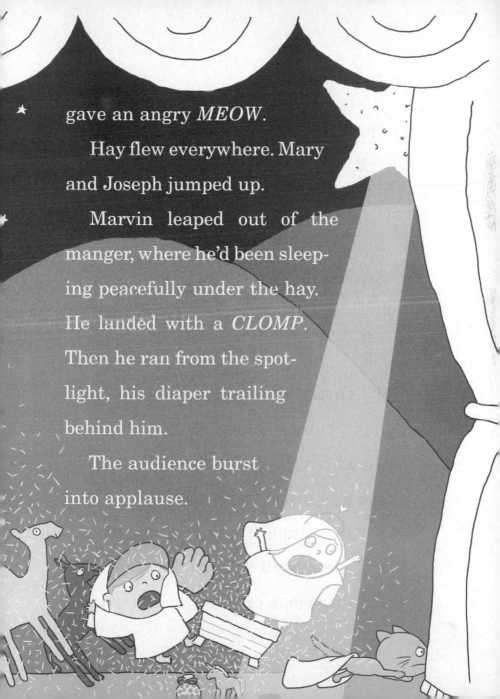

gave an angry *MEOW*.

Hay flew everywhere. Mary and Joseph jumped up.

Marvin leaped out of the manger, where he'd been sleeping peacefully under the hay. He landed with a *CLOMP*. Then he ran from the spotlight, his diaper trailing behind him.

The audience burst into applause.

The Grand Finale

The curtain closed. I scrambled back-stage, calling Marvin's name. That's when I felt the rush of cold air from the door and heard the traffic roaring by.

The stage lights flickered. I dragged myself back to the stage. The curtain swept open for the last time.

Ms. Marzipan wanted us to take a bow. Then Boris was supposed to step forward to thank everyone for coming and invite them to have cocoa and gingerbread in the cafeteria.

Only Boris never stepped forward. We bowed again. We looked around. Ms. Marzipan's smile started to get crooked. We bowed and bowed, and bowed again. Then Tonya curtsied and we all curtsied; even the boys wearing robes decided to curtsy. We didn't know what else to do.

BAM!

The back door slammed. Boris ran
up behind us and scampered to the
front of the stage. He was out of breath
and couldn't talk for a few seconds.

And his stomach looked *really* big.

"Thank you," he gasped. "Please join
us in the cafeteria for refreshments."
And then his stomach started wiggling
like crazy.

He turned around. When he spotted me, he unzipped his golden robe and laid Marvin in my arms.

"Praise Jesus, Jehovah, and Buddha, too," Mr. Bosco said from up on his ladder.

The audience lost it. The curtain closed quickly. The show was over.

"Boris, how did you find him?" I cried.

"I sneaked out during Yoshi's song to look for Steggo. I didn't see Steggo, but there was Marvin. Sitting on the sidewalk giving himself a bath."

"How did you ever get him to come to you?"

"I found an old cheese cracker in my

pocket. Cheese is his favorite food."

I laughed and kissed Marvin's head.

Then I saw Boris's miserable face.

Loo

king

up

A Miracle on Wheels

That evening freezing rain began to fall. But we all gathered outside anyway to admire the Periwinkle Tower.

Hunter hiked up the sidewalk to join us, and Sofie slid down. Pueblo del Mar shimmered with holiday lights. We skated on the slick driveway. We fell

and laughed. Even Tonya was happy. "Mr. Bosco fixed my pink LEDs!" she shouted.

Everyone was full of cheer except for Boris.

That's when the weirdest feeling came over me. I wanted Boris to be happy too. But I didn't know what to do. I slipped over beside him so that the brim of my hat protected his head from the rain.

Yoshi jumped up and down and pointed to the roof of the Periwinkle Tower. "I wish we had something to put up on the very top!"

"Something BIG," said Hunter.

"Something shiny," said Tonya.

"Something with a tail," added Sofie, galloping across the lawn in her riding boots.

OOOGA!

A horn blasted. Mr. Bosco's pickup truck sloshed up the drive. "Does anyone belong to this?" he shouted.

"Dr. Furr looked up from dinner, and this thing was staring at him through the window. He sees animals all day long, but this one nearly gave him a heart attack."

I looked at Boris. Boris looked at me. We smiled.

And then we both had exactly the same idea at exactly the same time.

Our Vacation

The freezing rain turned to snow. The whole week of vacation, we all had the best time playing together. Every day Sofie would ride her sled down to the tower, and Hunter would tromp up the hill.

On our second day of vacation Sofie

and I were building a snow cat behind the tower when we heard Yoshi give the emergency whistle. We ran into the lobby, where the others had already gathered.

A gigantic box had just arrived from Japan! It was full of presents from Santa. There was something for everyone.

A big tin of cocoa along with some cat stickers for me. Comic books wrapped up in a green jacket for Yoshi, a seashell mirror for Tonya. Sofie got a unicorn that turned into a horse when you removed its horn.

Hunter looked disappointed because

his present was so small. It took him forever to open it because of the baseball glove on his left hand. But when he finally managed to untape it, he jumped up and down, shouting: "Two tickets to the opening game!"

to: The kids at
the Periwinkle Tower
Pueblo del Mar
CA xoxox

from: SANTA

Boris got the most incredible gift: a real gum ball machine.

After he pocketed all the green ones, he set up the machine right there in the lobby by the red couch. That way when we got cold outside, we all could come in, sit down, and chew gum together.

Marvin loved his present too: a toy Swiss cheese with a mouse hidden inside.

Every evening during our vacation
we'd wind up in my apartment. I'd pop
open the big tin of cocoa and pass out
spoons. We'd stand in front of my window and watch the snow fall and eat
cocoa straight from the tin.

Sometimes Yoshi wore his new green jacket and played "Greensleeves" on his ukulele. Then when Sofie was about to fall asleep standing up, he'd play "Somewhere over the Rainbow," and everyone would slide down the banister and go home.

Take it from me: Things change.

Over the past month things had gone from bad to worse . . . to better and better.

P.S.

Wait—I almost forgot the most important part! For the first time in history, the Periwinkle Tower won the Pueblo del Mar Holiday Decorating Contest. All six of us, including Sofie and Hunter, got to shake the mayor's hand.

But there was only one medal.

We let Boris wear it.

I'm glad Boris moved into the tower. The two of us have plans. Plans to start an all-drum band. Plans to start a potato delivery service. Plans to start a gum club in the lobby.

It's funny. Boris and I really aren't alike at all. He loves caramels and I love chocolate-covered raisins. He has blond hair and I have dark hair. He wears stripes and I wear dots.

And he still gets on my last nerve.

But sometimes?

I feel like we're almost twins.